REAL AMERICAN GIRLS

❖ GIRLS ❖

❖

*Tell Their
Own Stories*

DOROTHY **and** THOMAS HOOBLER

REAL AMERICAN
GIRLS

*Tell Their
Own Stories*

Atheneum Books for Young Readers

Acknowledgments

We would like to thank Judy Belan of Augustana College Library, Carolyn Cole of the Los Angeles Public Library, Muir Dawson, Marjorie Houspian Dobkin, Kristin Eshelman of the Spencer Research Library at the University of Kansas, Chris Floerke of the Institute of Texan Cultures, Carol Spurlock Layman, Janice Madhu of the George Eastman House, Dr. Sadie Penzato, Judith A. Simonsen of the Milwaukee County Historical Society, Ken Skulski of the Immigrant City Archives, Christie Stanley of the Kansas State Historical Society, Kathleen Stocking of the New York State Historical Association, and Elizabeth Yates. All generously gave us their help in preparing this book.

Atheneum Books for Young Readers
An imprint of Simon & Schuster Children's Publishing Division
1230 Avenue of the Americas
New York, New York 10020

Book design by Nina Barnett

The text of this book is set in Bernhard Modern
Printed in the United States of America
10 9 8 7 6 5 4 3 2 1

Library of Congress Cataloging-in-Publication Data
Hoobler, Dorothy.
Real American girls tell their own stories / by Dorothy and Thomas Hoobler.
p.   cm.
Summary: Selections from autobiographical material written by American girls,
including one who lived in the colony of Virginia in 1756 and another who lived in
the early 1950s.
ISBN 0-689-82083-6
1. Girls—United States—History—Juvenile literature. 2. Girls—United States—
History—Sources—Juvenile literature. 3. Girls—United States—Biography—
Juvenile literature. [1. Women—Biography.] I. Hoobler, Thomas.
II. Title. HQ777.H76   1999   305.23—dc21   98-7993

FIRST
EDITION

CONTENTS

❧ INTRODUCTION ❧

In this book, you can read about the adventures of real American girls, as told by themselves. Some of the stories come from diaries, one is from a letter, and others are from autobiographies that the girls wrote when they grew up. The diaries are printed here just the way they were written—including the misspellings.

The earliest story is from 1756, by a girl who lived in the colony of Virginia, and the latest is from the early 1950s. Nobody in these stories had a television or a computer or ever played a video game.

But they still had fun—in ways that might surprise you. And sometimes (just like girls today) they got into trouble, were teased in school, and had crushes on boys. One girl even wondered about life in the year 2000.

She couldn't see forward into the future. But in this book you can look back into the past. Although life was different then, people were much the same as today. We hope you'll find girls here that you would have liked as friends.

1

❧ BEST FRIENDS ❧

*C*atherine Elizabeth Havens grew up in New
York City in the 1840s. In those days, the city was
very different than it is today. Farmhouses stood
where there are now skyscrapers, and two-thirds of
Manhattan Island was still woods and farmland.
Families in the "city" part of Manhattan lived in three-
and four-story houses, instead of apartments.

Catherine was the youngest of her father's fourteen
children. He had married a second time after his first
wife died. Some of Catherine's half brothers and
sisters were grown up with children of their own, and
she enjoyed visiting them. In fact, her best friend,
Ellen, was also her niece. In the fall of 1840, Ellen
came to the city to visit Catherine. The two girls were

fond of pranks, but as Catherine's diary shows, sometimes the tables were turned on them.

December 8

Ellen is here and we have fun. We have been down to Staten Island to [visit] one of my sisters. She has ice cream on Thursdays so we try to go then. One day I ate it so fast it gave me a pain in the forehead and my brother-in-law said I must warm it over the register and I did and it all melted and then they all laughed and said he was joking but he gave me some more. . . .

December 10

Ellen and I went shopping alone. We went to Bond's Dry Goods Store on Sixth Avenue just below Ninth Street to buy a yard of calico to make an apron for Maggie's birthday. We hope she will like it. It is good quality, for we pulled the corner and twitched it as we have seen our mothers do and it did not tear. Ellen and I call each other Sister Cynthia and Sister Juliana, and when we bought the calico Ellen said, "Sister Cynthia, have you any change? I have only a fifty-dollar bill papa left me this morning," and the clerk laughed. I guess he knew Ellen was making it up.

Sometimes we play I am blind and Ellen leads me along on the street and once a lady went by and said to her little girl, "See that poor child, she is blind," and perhaps when I get old I may be really blind as a punishment for pretending. . . .

I hope Ellen will stay all winter. She is full of pranks and smarter than I am [even] if she is younger and I hope we will have lots of snow. When there is real good sleighing my sister hires a stage sleigh and takes me and a lot of my schoolmates [on] a sleigh ride down Broadway to the Battery and back. The sleigh is open and very long and has long seats on each side and straw on the floor to keep our feet warm and the sleigh bells sound so cheerful. . . .

January 2, 1850

Yesterday was New Year's Day, and I had lovely presents. We had 39 callers and I have an ivory tablet and I write all their names down in it. We have to be dressed and ready by ten o'clock to receive [visitors].

Some of the gentlemen come together and don't stay more than a minute; but some go into the back room and take some oysters and coffee and cake and stay and talk. My cousin is always the first to come, and sometimes he comes before we are ready and we find him sitting behind the door on the end of the sofa because he is bashful. . . .

Next January we shall be half through the nineteenth century. I hope I shall live to see the next century but I don't want to be alive when the year 2000 comes, for my Bible teacher says the world is coming to an end then, and perhaps sooner.

Catherine got her wish. She lived until 1939, when she was nearly 100 years old.

❖

*M*artha Carey Thomas, born in Baltimore in 1857, started her diary at the age of thirteen. She called it "the private diary of Jo March." Jo March was a character in a book that had just been published— Little Women, *by Louisa May Alcott. Martha had obviously made Jo March her heroine, and indeed, she was very much like Jo. She loved to read, but always worried that she wasn't reading enough serious books. At the end of 1871, she wrote in her diary, "This year I have only read 8 useful books and 55 novels. What am I coming to, just think of it."*

Though her family was wealthy, Martha was not a conventional girl. She was as lively and bold as a girl could be in those days. She wrote, "People seem to think that girls don't want any fun, and [if girls] want to row and climb they are shocked and say it isn't LADYLIKE. But B [Bess King, her best friend] and I are going to resist to the last!!"

The following entries from Martha's diary describe one of the hilarious "experiments" she and Bess carried out.

November 25 [1870]

Have come across such a glorious book called 'Boys Play Book of Science.' Am going to read it through and see if whether ain't some experiments Bess and I can try. Won't it be jolly if we really can? But it takes money money money even for the privilege of blowing one's self up. . . .

November 26

Set a mouse trap last night in case Bess and I might want to get his skeleton. Caught him but he wasn't dead. Neither Julie [a maid] nor Netty [the cook] would kill him so I heroically dropped the trap in a pail of water and rushed out of the room. Then took my slippers into Mother's room . . . and sewed sewed sewed. . . .

Pretty soon I heard someone calling "Min" and

knew it must be Bess 'cause no one else ever calls me "Min." Well first we roasted some chestnuts then proceeded to the more important duty of getting to skeleton of a mouse. The poor fellow being drowned by this time we took our victim out in yard, bared our glittering knives and commenced operations. But the horrid mouse's fur was so soft that we couldn't make a hole and besides it made us sick and our hands trembled so we couldn't do a thing. But concluding it was *feminine* nonsense we made a hole and squeezed his insides out. It was the most disgusting thing I ever did. We then took off his skin. It came off elegantly just like a glove, and then holding it by the tail we chased poor Julie all around. She was so afraid of it just as if it were even worse than a chicken and [we] finally put it on the fire to boil to Julie's great disgust. When it had boiled we took it again and picked all the meat off it and saved its tongue and eyes to look [at] through the

microscope and then the mouse looked like a real skeleton. We then put it out the window to bleach and then as Bess had to go I walked with her. . . .

When I got home I found that Netty had thrown away our tongue and eyes, and worst of all woe woe is me that our skeleton that had taken us 3 mortal hours to get, had fallen out of the window and smashed. Oh Science! Why will thou not protect thy votaries? [worshippers]

In the afternoon lolled around learnt Greek and sewed everlasting slippers. Bess said when she told her father about our getting the mouse he looked grave and said, Bessie Bessie thee is losing all thy *feminine* traits. I'm afraid I haven't got any to lose for I greatly prefer cutting up mice to sewing.

❖

Kathie Gray started a diary in 1876, when she was twelve. One of her first entries tells about a visit *from her good friend Jessie. The two girls slept in four-poster canopy beds, which suggested a game.*

Then Mama came and tucked us up in bed and kissed us Goodnight. Dear Mama she loves to have us so happy. Then we named the bed posts each the name of any boy we liked. The one we looked at first in the morning would be our fate. [That is, he would be the person they would marry.] The big girls do this. Of coarse its silly but just for fun. Jessie said she didn't know but one nice boy and that was her cousin Johnnie he didn't plage [plague, or tease] one all the time. So she named *all* her posts for him. We both feel so sorry I haven't any brother and she hasnt eather. If we had one which ever had him we would see he married the other one for we *SO* want to be related. That would make us *in laws* any way. Then Mama wrapped [rapped on the door] and said "Go to sleap Girlies" so we did.

❖

Sometimes, even best friends get into fights. That happened to Devorah Major and her friend Lora. Devorah described it in her memoir of growing up in San Francisco in the 1950s.

The first time I met Lora she was getting her hair pressed. Her mother had just singed a lock, and the bright yellow kitchen smelled of oil and dry smoke as it crackled. Whining, Lora pulled away as her ear collided with the thick slate-gray comb. I was a welcome relief. . . .

Lora had more than a little spunk. While the hot comb made her mean, the music in her home made her swirl. She was for me a wonder. She could hula-hoop from her neck, do one-arm cartwheels, and blow gum bubbles as large as her head. . . .

Lora and I never fought, or when we did, it wasn't for long. I suppose that could have been because we were two of the few black girls in the neighborhood, but I think it was because I was peaceable and she was fun. Other than our hair— mine was wild and "good," impossibly messy most of the time; hers was kinky and "bad," excruciatingly neat even on the windiest days— we really had little about which to argue. But one day we found something which was just big enough to set up a spark and we, with cajoling from my brother and hisses from her sister, entered the garage where we began to wail at each other, pulling hair and circling around each other as our siblings rooted us on, offering tips for tight punches, hard kicks and good slaps. They laughed and would not allow us to stop the fight although I stood biting my lips and wincing, forgetting what the issue had been but knowing I was supposed to be mad and trying hard to show it.

And then we didn't speak for a long time. . . .

After a respectable spell it was over. After a number of days of not playing together at recess, not walking home with each other, not skating together, not borrowing each other's skate key, not searching the gutters for lost pennies, and not having a best friend, we were friends again. We were sitting on the stoop. I finally had gotten the wide petticoat I had pined for. Lora already had three. "Come on," she said as I lifted my dress to show the lace, and she took me by the hand to her dining room at the back of the flat, where no one seemed to ever eat, except on Christmas or Easter, and where the record player lived. She put on a forty-five and we began to dance. First we twirled around the table as the cloth swirled and floated above our ashy legs. Leaping and prancing we performed circles around the wide oak table and began to spin each other under and around each other's arms playing the record again and again, melting in giggles at our fantasy dance hall. Oiling the floor, we were little girls reaching to be women, laughing as our skirts flew around our spindle legs as her father's record beat out lick after lick of happy talk.

➤ SCHOOL DAYS ➤

Instead of going to school, suppose you had a tutor who came to your house. Imagine you had to start your classes even before you had breakfast! That was what life was like for Maria Carter, who lived on a Virginia estate in colonial times. If the following letter that Maria wrote to her cousin can be believed, her life was like that every day of the year. But maybe Maria was just in a bad mood and exaggerating. At any rate, the cousin certainly didn't get the "Merry & Comical" letter she had asked Maria for!

March 25, 1756

My Dear Cousin:

You have rea'y [really] imposed a Task upon me which I can by no means perform viz: [which is]

that of writing a Merry & Comical Letter: how
shou'd [I] my dear that am ever Confined either at
School or with my Grandmama know how the
World goes on? Now I will give you the History
of one Day the Repetition of which without
variations carries me through the Three hundred
and sixty five Days, which you know compleats the
year. Well then first begin, I am awakened out of a
sound Sleep with some croaking voice either Patty's,
Milly's, or some other of our Domestics [servants]
with Miss Polly Miss Polly get up, tis time to rise,
Mr. Price [her tutor] is down Stairs, and tho' I hear
them I lie quite snugg till my Grandmama uses her
Voice, then up I get, huddle on my cloaths & down
to Book, then to Breakfast, then to School again, &
may be I have an Hour to my self before Dinner,
then the Same Story over again till twi-light, &
then a small portion of time before I go to rest and
so you must expect nothing from me but that I am

Dear Cousin, Most Affectionately Yours,
Maria Carter

❖

*W*hen Cornelia Raymond was thirteen, she
went to the Poughkeepsie Female Academy, a school
for girls. You will probably find her story about the
academy hard to believe. For this took place in 1874,
when many words that we consider harmless today
were regarded as improper, especially for female ears.
Legs, for example, were supposed to be referred to as
limbs. As Cornelia explained in her autobiography,
even the word pants could cause an uproar.

Good little girl as I was I had one humiliating
experience. I happened to open the door in the hall
to find a ragged man, who asked for a pair of pants.
Returning to the schoolroom . . . I found myself
utterly unable to explain . . . the needs of the man
at the door. After declaring several times, "Oh, Miss
Bascom, I cannot tell you what he wants," I finally
cried in agony, "He wants a pair of pants," at which
the school broke forth into shrieks of laughter.

At the close of school a few days later, as we were singing a hymn, we came to these words: "So a soul that's born of God pants to view his lovely face." Marion Jones [who sat next to her] pointed to the word "pants." I laughed, dropped my head, and then looked up to see Dr. Wright and all the teachers glaring at me. An awful silence was broken by this dreadful question from Dr. Wright. "Nellie, what do you find funny in the hymn?" In cowardice born of agony I murmured, "Marion made me laugh." Fortunately Marion was less sensitive and to the same question replied, with nose in the air, "Impossible to tell you here." We were told to come to his study, but I think he realized the probable impropriety of what we had to tell him. The incident ended by his saying that until we could show a spirit of reverence we need not join in the hymn. I wept all night, and from that moment never opened my lips in the closing exercises.

❖

*D*o you think you'd like to be rich?
*Consuelo Vanderbilt, born in 1877, was a member of
one of the country's richest families. She lived in
houses that were like palaces; one had "a colossal
playroom where we used to bicycle and roller skate
with our cousins and friends." But Consuelo
remembered parts of her childhood as being miserable.*

Sitting up straight was one of the crucial tests
of ladylike behavior. A horrible instrument was
devised which I had to wear when doing my
lessons. It was a steel rod which ran down my
spine and was strapped at my waist and over
my shoulders—another strap went around my
forehead to the rod. I had to hold my book high
when reading, and it was almost impossible to
write in so uncomfortable a position. However, I
probably owe my straight back to those many
hours of discomfort.

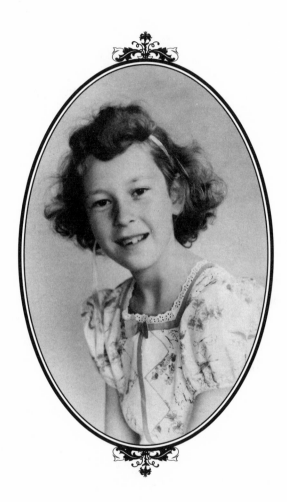

❖

Mary Paxson started a diary in 1880, when she was eight years old. Her family lived in a small town north of Philadelphia. Though Mary's spelling is often faulty, her writing is direct and lively. She put one of her school assignments in her diary.

February 21 (1881), and I am 9 years old today it is my Birthday thats why, and tomorrow is George Washingtons Birthday only he is not living and I am. He is to old to be living thats why, and tomorrow at school my class has to make an essay about him, an essay is when you write about things. I mean each of us must write one apiece and we musent copy it out of any history books and our Fathers and our Mothers musent help us either and it musent be longer than 130 words or shorter either, and it must be personal, I asked Mamma how to spell personal

and what it means and this is what I wrote,
[Each of the following 130 words has a number
over it in the diary:]

"George Washington was tall and not very
good looking, he had large hands and a large
nose, any way they look big in the pitchures.
When he was 13 years old he made 110 rules for
himself to use to learn how to be polite and to
behave well. Maybe when I am 13 years old I will
make some too only I dont believe I will need
so many. 25 or 30 will be enough I guess. He
married Martha Custis and she had been married
once before and had plenty of money. He died of
laryngittis and I have had it twice and never died
yet. He went to the grave Childless that means he
had no children, the only thing he was Father to
was his country."

That's all I could write for it took all of my
130 words. Papa says there isent any doubt about
its being personal enough. . . .

❖

Did you ever have a teacher you really liked? Helen MacKnight (called "Nellie") remembered how her life was changed by a teacher. Born in 1872, Helen had a sad childhood. Her father left the family to search for gold in the West, and her mother was forced to take a job in a factory. But as Helen recalled,

In school I found happiness, for there was smiling Miss House, Addie House. Among all the names that I have known and forgotten, that name is fresh in my memory. I thought she was beautiful. Her hair was brown, and she wore it in brushed-over-the-finger curls that fell to her waist; the front hair was caught up with a ribbon just as Mama combed mine, and she wore a fringe on her forehead. Her eyes were kind and brown and sunny, but best of all, she read to us every day from Hans Andersen's Fairy Tales.

The first story she selected was the Snow
Queen, and I listened to it breathlessly, afraid
to stir lest I should lose one word. When she
finished the story, she told us that she was giving
the book to the pupil in her grade who made the
best marks in arithmetic.

I was nine years old, and I don't remember
ever having wanted anything desperately up
till that time. But right then a resolve formed
itself in my brain that made my heart beat with
high endeavor. Addition, subtraction, and
multiplication tables became the end and aim of
all existence. But there was a girl in the class who
had a genius for figures. She really liked to add
and subtract and do her tables. The class were on
her side. I was not a favorite. I was too well
washed and brushed and dressed to fit in with
their democratic ideas; besides, they considered
me teacher's pet. . . .

But I did my sums heroically, always a lap
behind the other girl but always hoping that a

miracle might happen, and it did! A week before school closed in the spring, she came down with the measles and had to stay out of school. The prize came to me. In the precious volume Miss House wrote:

> *Reward of merit*
> *Nellie Mattie MacKnight*
> *Never give up the ship*

Helen MacKnight let that motto guide her through many tragic events and hardships, which she described in her autobiography. When she wrote it in 1934, she could look back on a successful career as one of the first women doctors in the United States.

❖

*O*f course, teasing and bullying were also part of people's school-days memories. Being "different" was one way to attract unwanted attention. In both of the *stories below, the difference was that the girls could not speak English.*

Helen Rosen's parents immigrated to the United States from Germany in the 1880s. Helen and her sister Dolly were born here, but their parents spoke German at home. This caused problems when it came time for the girls to go to school. Because German immigrants referred to themselves as Deutsch (which means "German"), English-speaking Americans nicknamed them "Dutch."

The first day at school was not too good. Although I had been born in New York, until I was five years old I knew not one word of English. There were no kindergartens. At six I went to the primary school. Dolly began on the same day. By that time we had a few English words, but only a few. German was the language of the house. Mama and Papa spoke

German to each other and to us. When we came out of school that day the other children called after us, "Dutchy, Dutchy, can't speak muchy." Dolly and I ran home, up the three flights of stairs and into the kitchen where Mama was putting out milk and bread for us on the table. Dolly burst into tears, and I burst into speech. "They called us Dutchy. Can't speak muchy!"

"Never mind," Mama said, "I'll make you some cocoa." She did not know what else to do about it, but when Papa came home she told him and he said, "Not another word of German will I ever speak to one of you. If all you can manage to know is one language, it better be English." And from that day on he spoke only English to us. Mama kept on speaking German, but we answered her in English.

❖

Mary Paik Lee was born in Korea in 1900, but her family came to the United States when she was six. She and her older brother Meung went to the public school in Riverside, California. Mary did not have happy memories of their arrival.

My first day at school was a very frightening experience. As we entered the schoolyard, several girls formed a ring around us, singing a song and dancing in a circle. When they stopped, each one came over to me and hit me in the neck, hurting and frightening me. They ran away when a tall woman came toward us. Her bright yellow hair and big blue eyes looking down at me were a fearful sight; it was my first close look at such a person. She was welcoming me to her school, but I was frightened. When she addressed me, I answered in Korean, "I don't understand you." I turned around, ran all the way home, and hid in our shack. Father laughed when he heard about my behavior. He told me there was nothing to be afraid of; now that we were living here in America, where everything is different from Korea, we would have to learn to get along with everyone.

The next day when I went to school with my brother, the girls did not dance around us; I guess the teacher must have told them not to do it. I learned later that the song they sung was

Ching Chong, Chinaman,
Sitting on a wall.
Along came a white man,
And chopped his head off.

The last line was the signal for each girl to "chop my head off" by giving me a blow on the neck. That must have been the greeting they gave to all the Oriental kids who came to school the first day.

❧ IN TROUBLE ❦

Clara Barton was the founder of the American Red Cross. In her memoir of her childhood, Barton recalls some of the incidents that inspired her to become a nurse. In one of these, she was not the nurse, but the patient. In 1831, when she was ten, Clara's family lived on a farm, where she and three male cousins enjoyed playing together.

There was, and still is, directly in front of the house, a small circular, natural pond [which] in winter becomes a thing of beauty and a joy forever to the skater. . . . The boys were all fine skaters; I wanted to skate, too, but skating had not then become customary, in fact, not even allowable for

girls; and when, one day, my father saw me sitting on the ice attempting to put on a pair of skates, he seemed shocked . . . and said something about "tomboys." But this did not cure my desire; nor could I understand why it was not as well for me to skate as for the boys; I was as strong, could run as fast and ride better, indeed they would not have presumed to approach me [in skill] with a horse. Neither could the boys understand it, and this misconception led them into an error and me into trouble.

One clear, cold, starlight Sunday morning, I heard a low whistle under my open chamber window. I realized that the boys were out for a skate and wanted to communicate with me. On going to the window, they informed me that they had an extra pair of skates and if I could come out they would put them on me and "learn" me how to skate. It was Sunday morning; no one would be up till late, and the ice was so smooth and "glare." The stars were bright, the temptation was too great. I was in my dress in a moment and out. The skates were fastened on firmly, one of the boys' wool neck "comforters" tied about my waist, to be held by the boy in front. The other two were to stand on either side, and at a signal the cavalcade started. Swifter and swifter we went, until at length we reached a spot where the ice had been cracked and was full of sharp edges. These threw me, and the speed with which we were progressing, and the distance before we could quite come to a stop, gave terrific opportunity for cuts and wounded knees. . . . There was more blood flowing than any of us had ever seen. Something must be done. Now all of the wool neck comforters came into requisition; my wounds were bound up, and I was helped into the house, with one knee of ordinary respectable cuts and bruises; the other frightful. . . .

We decided to all keep silent [about what had happened]; but how to conceal the limp? I must have no limp, but walk well. I managed breakfast

without notice. Dinner not quite so well, and I had to acknowledge that I had slipped down and hurt my knee a little. This gave my limp more latitude, but the next day it was so decided [obvious], that I was held up and searched. It happened that the best knee was inspected; the stiff wool comforter soaked off, and a suitable dressing given it. This was a great relief, as it offered pretext for my limp, no one observing that I limped with the wrong knee.

But the other knee [did not heal] . . . and finally had to be revealed. The result was a surgical dressing and my foot held up in a chair for three weeks, during which time I read the "Arabian Nights" from end to end. . . .

Twenty-five years later, when on a visit to the old home . . . I saw my father, then a grey-haired grandsire, out on the same little pond, fitting the skates carefully to the feet of his little twin granddaughters, holding them up to make their first start in safety, I remembered my wounded knees, and blessed the great Father that progress and change were among the possibilities of His people.

I never learned to skate. When it became fashionable I had neither time nor opportunity.

❖

Rachel Q. Buttz was born in Indiana in 1850. As the youngest child in a large family, she was babied and coddled by her older sisters and brothers. When Rachel was about eight years old, her cousin Ruth came to visit. Rachel recalled the drastic effect of a thoughtless comment.

I suppose Cousin Ruth thought I was vain of my golden curls which visitors always admired; so, to give me something else to think about, she teased me one day about the size and shape of my nose. I never knew until then that it was any use to think about my nose, except to keep it clean; so I was astonished to learn that the size and shape of the nose might spoil the beauty of a face. . . . But I firmly believed that there was no defect that could not be cured; so I confided to Mary [a sister] that my nose would be *pretty* the next morning. I was quite sure that one night's application of my contemplated remedy would prove effectual. I provided myself with a strong flax thread, and . . . I gathered up my nose with a firm hand, wrapped the thread around it many times, and then tying it securely, I soon slept in peace. In the morning my nose did not feel well; but I had been told that "to cure, medicine must hurt"; so I bore it patiently. Without complaint I allowed Mary to remove the thread from my swollen and injured member, while she said consolingly that my nose *had* improved. Of course a laugh went around the family circle on account of the treatment I had given to my poor nose, yet all were sorry for me, and I suppose none more sorry than she who had caused the

trouble. Mother forbade such teasing, and I heard nothing more about it, but all through my early girlhood, I was extremely sensitive about the size and shape of my nose. I imagined that always when I was introduced to strangers, their first mental comment was, "What an ugly nose!" and I never became entirely reconciled to my prominent feature until I began to mingle with the world and found that among many other unhandsome noses, mine passed unnoticed. In time, I became not only satisfied with this useful organ, but very thankful that I had just such a nose.

❖

Caroline Richards and her younger sister Anna lived with their grandparents in a small town in New York State. Caroline's grandmother was particularly religious, and sometimes the children didn't meet her expectations. When Caroline was twelve, she noted this in her diary.

Sunday, August 10, 1854

Reverend Mr. Daggett's text this morning [at the church service] was, "Remember the Sabbath day to keep it holy." Grandmother said she thought the sermon did not do us much good for she had to tell us several times this afternoon to stop laughing. Grandmother said we ought to be good Sundays if we want to go to heaven, for there it is one eternal Sabbath. Anna said she didn't want to be an angel just yet and I don't think there is the least danger of it, as far as I can judge.

❖

Kathie Gray had just started her diary in 1876, when she recorded an overnight visit from her friend Jessie. Kathie lived with her mother, aunt, and grandmother in Ohio. Her spelling was not perfect, but her sense of humor is on target.

April 29, 1876

When I was about seven my favorite Bible
Story was about Joseph and his coat of many
colors and his getting to be a ruler and so nobly
saving his brothers who had been so mean to him
when there was an awful famine in the country
where they lived. How they were going to starve to
death and he gave them corn to make bread. Well
I always loved bread and butter espeshally the way
Mama fixed it for me sometimes, with scraped
maple sugger on it and sprinkles of cream on top
of that.

Um-m-m that makes me hungry just writing it
down even right after breakfast. I always hated
crusts but I was supposed to eat them of course.
Then I had a bright idea. I thought I would *save
every crust* of my between meals lunches—save
them all safely in the Grandma tea set which
nobody looks at only once in a long while and
then when we had a famine in our country—as
we might have most any time—I would climb up

in the cubbard and bring out these crusts and say
See my starving family what I have saved for you.
Then they would fall on my neck as they did on
Josephs in the Bible and say O Kathie wasn't that
wonderful of you and other starving folks would
wish *their* little girl had saved her bread crusts for
the days of famine. Well it was a lovely plan but it
didn't work for when Aunt Mary was hurrying to
get down the dishes because the new minister was
coming to tea she found the sugger bowl, tea pot
and every covered dish crammed full of moulded
crusts—awfully moulded and smelly. She felt
cross and gave me a shaking. Even now when I
am twelve I think that was too bad for I really
tried to do a nobel deed (as well as get rid of eat-
ing crusts until I had to) and I neerly broke my
neck more than once climbing up in a hurry to
hide them before any boddy came in.

✤

Eleanor Hallowell Abbott grew up in Cambridge, Massachusetts, in the 1880s. She came from an old and distinguished New England family. But hot-tempered Eleanor didn't quite fit into the family mold.

My brother Edward Apthorp was a terrible tease. Nothing could break him of it. One day in almost maniacal rage at some latest phase of his tormenting, I just stood back with flaming face and clenched fists and called him a *fool*. My father came hurrying with his Bible and read me the passage where it said, "Whosoever calleth his brother a fool is in danger of hell-fire." This sobered me at once but did not satisfy me. Without delay I ran off to the shed and returned with a hammer. "And what will happen to me," I questioned, "if I only kill him with a hammer?"

❖

*G*oing to fairs in the summertime was a thrill for most nineteenth-century children. But tricksters and con artists sometimes waited at fairs to take your money. Helen MacKnight remembered the time she was swindled at a New York State fair in the 1880s, when she was about twelve.

I thought I would buy some peanuts with the money I had, but I passed a place where a man was yelling, "Right this way for the jungle. Lions, tigers, and monkeys straight from their native haunts. Every lady who goes into this show will be given a ring on her way out!"

Inside the crowded tent were three or four cages with a lion, a tiger, three monkeys, and a leopard. They were listless and sick and discouraged looking, and even the trainer, with his whip, had difficulty in getting them to get up and pace back and forth for the benefit of those who had paid an entrance fee. I felt sorry for the animals; I did not want to watch them. I went back outside and walked up to the high platform where the man stood, and told him I wanted my ring. He said, "Why yes, sure, always glad to please the ladies." He took up a big bell on a stand in front of him and reached down and rang it in my face. Everybody laughed as though it was a great joke. Then I saw the whole thing as a cheat, and my face burned with shame and indignation.

❖

Kathleen Cannell was about six years old when her brother Bud took her to Sunday school. This was around 1897 in New York City. The results were such a disaster that Kathleen didn't have to go back for two years.

Muds [her mother] gave me a dime to put in the collection plate. As I had seen her do with dollar bills, I promptly put it in my stocking. Mine were attached under my fat knees with . . . beribboned garters. . . . I knelt down quietly for prayers, listened attentively to the exciting story of David and Goliath, and thanked the teacher prettily for the illuminated text [a card with a picture of a Bible passage on it] of Daniel in the Lions' Den, though Bud shushed me when I tried to show him the "lovely kitties."

"S'me-ee," I hissed, pointing to the girlish figure of Daniel, apparently in his nightie, with long curls. . . . "S'me and my cats."

"'Tis not; 's Daniel," Bud whispered firmly, buttoning the card in his breast pocket.

It was at that moment the collection plate was passed. I began to grope frantically for my dime, which, of course, had slipped down into my red strap-slipper. My fist got caught under my garter and Bud had to take that off for me. Anxious to avoid a scandal, he made signs to the sidesman to pass along, but I howled: "Wait, wait. Muddie gave me ten cents; I must give it to God."

In my confusion I took off the wrong shoe and

stocking and insisted upon putting them on again before I took off the others. A distinct revulsion of Public Opinion was noticeable. Ladies who had gently cooed over "the tiny darling," turned tight-lipped. The sidesman glared down horribly over a red handle-bar mustache. Bud was crimson, and I'm sure only the idea that he must keep up his prestige in front of me prevented him from crying like a girl. At last I triumphantly shook out the dime, which rolled away down the aisle. Probably fearing further demonstrations on my part, the sidesman actually bent to pick it up. It was unfortunate that my teacher should have had the same idea. They shocked foreheads like a couple of bull moose, and she came up for air looking groggy, with her ostrich toque [hat] askew. The sidesman, however, had got the coin. He put it in the plate with such dignity as he could muster.

Bud refused to speak to me all the way home, though I tried to make light conversation. I was not sent to Sunday school again for nearly two years.

JUST HAVING FUN

Edwina Fallis was born in Denver in 1876, only nine years after a trapper built the first cabin there. Edwina recalled the pleasures that each season of the year brought to the children of the little town.

The things that we found on the way to school. What a world of wonder and beauty they opened up to us! The soft dust that felt good to our feet and sparkled in the sun at half past eight of a December morning. At half past eleven that same day the world outside was gray and the school room so dark you couldn't see the fine line your slate pencil made on your slate as you tried to print "CAT." But you didn't care for that for your

eyes were glued to the window where the blizzard whirled the icy snowflakes against the glass with a cold tinkling sound. Then the mothers began to come and stand around in the big hall. Ethel May cried for fear her Mama would forget to come but I didn't worry. I knew Mama would get me home if she had to go to the North Pole for me. . . .

In the month of May I might find a piece of broken shell, robin's egg blue, under the tree with the bird's nest. The tiny pebbles, all of a size that we gathered by handfuls off the top of the ant hills. We had to do it in a hurry and not stoop down to do it for fear the big red ants would walk up our clothes and sting us. I wouldn't blame them. They had to defend their castles. There were the catkins, red, yellow, and green tassels that fell from the cottonwood trees onto the sidewalks and lay curled around like the figures in Mama's Paisley shawl. The tassels that hung on the tree long enough made cotton balls. The boys could climb up the tree to get the cotton balls to shoot in their pea shooters. Sometimes they got more than their pockets would hold and gave the overflow to us girls. We would hide them in our desks, if the teacher did not see them first, and take them home after school to string for a doll's necklace. . . . When all the cotton balls on all the lady cottonwood trees in Denver dried out there was a big snowstorm. Only this kind of snow didn't melt and that was the reason why grown folks didn't like cottonwoods. We children loved them.

In the fall we would fasten the round shiny yellow leaves together with their stems and wear them as crowns. The Autumn winds would send the leaves fluttering down until they lay thick on the ground. We liked to shuffle through the leaves and rake them into piles in the dry ditch beside the carriage step. It was fun to jump from the high carriage step to the dry leaves and fairly bury ourselfs.

After all this would come the bon-fires. We would fill gunny sacks, the wheelbarrow, and the little express wagon and tote them all over to the vacant lot across the street. There they must lie until there was no wind stirring. . . . Oh, the smell, the bitter, woodsy smell of burning leaves. It lifted you out of yourself and took you back to the time when you were an Indian princess or a gypsie, or a wild wood fairy. Was it any wonder that Denver children loved their cottonwoods?

❖

Delfina Cuero's people were Digu</sub>eños, Native Americans who lived in California. Born around 1900, Delfina recalled the games she and the other children played.

Matilda Osun was a good friend. . . . Matilda and I used to make dolls of rags and stuff them with manure and use sticks for legs. We made clay dolls and animals also. We didn't put them in a fire to make them hard, so they would fall to

pieces after a while. We made a lot of mud dolls with stones pushed into a slit made with a stick for eyes. . . .

We used to have wars against the boys. I can remember how crazy we were. We used to have wars with them with xamca [wild gourds], throwing them at each others' heads. We could have cut someone or put out each others' eyes. We didn't think about that then, we had so much fun. I've been hit many times in the head but we all had a good time. Sometimes boys and girls would be on both teams and other times it would be boys against girls. Sometimes it would end in a big fight and everybody would get mad. If someone got hurt we would get mad and have a real fight, but we were all right the next day—friends again. The gourds were round and hard, like hard balls. . . .

We had a lot of fun with all kinds of games. We played hockey with a watas [stick] and a ball and a goal. Our ball was made out of sticks. We shot bows and arrows and threw xampu [rabbit sticks] at targets. My father made me a rabbit stick [a curved flattened stick similar to a boomerang] but I wasn't very good with it. The old folks made little bows and arrows for us. Even the girls used them and learned to throw rabbit sticks. Some girls were good.

We used to make sticks for horses and ride those. We didn't have any toys to play with. We made our own things. . . .

Besides wrestling when we were young, we used to have fun sliding down smooth rocks. I ruined my rear end one time I slid down the rocks so much. We used to have races too. I used to outrun Fernando Quaha. He is older than I am, too. I don't know about now though, he might outrun me now.

We used to get on the highest rocks and jump down to see who was brave. We used to play rough. Sometimes someone would push another off and someone would break an arm or get hurt. But most of the time, when we played we had fun.

We didn't have a lot of time to play. Most of the time I went with my mother and gathered greens to eat.

❖

Kathleen Cannell's brother Bud forgave her for disgracing him in Sunday school (p. 51). In a few years, they had another brother and sister to play with. The four were reckless in their adventures. Kathleen remembered the fun they had while living in their grandfather's house near Lake Ontario.

Grandpa Wilson had fitted up a gymnasium with every then-known appliance. Almost before Jamie and Sue could walk they were racing each other by their hands along the suspended ladders. Bud and I were their trainers. We put them through it and they liked it. Every day we made them exercise with Indian clubs and iron dumbbells which they could hardly heft. We

invented "Human Bowling," with the little kids as the balls. They idea was for them to do cartwheels right down the bowling alley . . . and knock over the ninepins, while the others bet marbles on their favorites. Skinning the cat in the dangling giant rings and hanging by our feet from the horizontal pole was soon really child's play to all of us. Bud and I worked out a "Death defying Aerial Act"—it nearly was the death of Grandpa Wilson when he saw it. Swinging on trapezes hung from two central beams, we would change places in the air, then swing by our knees and grab by the ankle Jamie and Sue, respectively, balanced in iron rings at either end. While we were practicing, we occasionally dropped our unfortunate stooges. There was no net, but the gym wasn't very high and they fell onto the thick practice mats we used for wrestling. At that, it's a wonder we didn't all dash out what brains we had.

Carol Spurlock Layman grew up in the town of Vernon, Indiana, during the 1940s. What she liked to do best was roller-skate. She and her friends wore the old-fashioned skates that attached to your regular shoes and had metal wheels. To put them on right, you needed a skate key, as Carol describes. But then the fun began!

Every Vernon girl had to own a pair of roller skates if she didn't own another store-bought toy. We could feel our little pulses beating every time we clamped those skates to the soles of our oxfords. (Skating was one of the few activities worth the sacrifice of putting on socks and shoes in the summer.) Our skates were silver-colored steel, made well enough to be passed down through the family.

Once we adjusted them to fit our shoes, we used a skate key to lock them in place. A skate key was not like any other key. One end was flat

with a hexagon hole for lengthening the skates.
The other end was a square for adjusting the steel
clamps that curved up around the fronts of our
shoes. Because we had to carry the key with us to
tighten or remove the skates, there was a slot in it
for slipping it onto the leather strap that went
around our ankles. Most of us kept our keys
hanging around our necks, on strings that were
once white.

Katie and I usually skated together, starting
our route with the courthouse square. The
sidewalk there was better than the others in town
and most of it was level. Here we could take those
long, gliding warm-up strides . . . one foot, then
the other. Our wheels clicked across the cracks
like locomotives clicked over the rails when they
slowed down for the depot.

The courthouse square also was a good place
for speed skating, for leaning from side to side
taking short, fast strokes until our keys were
flying back and forth and bruising our shoulder

blades. We liked to do this on the highway side to impress the drivers.

By now we were feeling tough, so it was time for other parts of town, for the Rogers curve, where the squares [of concrete that made up the sidewalk] leaned in all directions and slanted up and around, dangerously close to the highway. The sidewalk at the Rogers curve was like a roller coaster, something we had seen in pictures.

Van Gorden's hill was dangerous too. Starting at Jackson's, it was a fast drop, with the highway waiting at the bottom beneath concrete steps. Sometimes we had to choose between a deliberate fall and skinned knees and elbows or flying out in front of a semi [truck].

We knew every inch of those sidewalks. We knew when to get ready for a smooth square next to an aggravate [aggregate, or rough-stoned] square, and the fun contrast of sounds that came from our wheels when we hit one right after the other. We had no respect for any . . . chalk

markings, any leftover hopscotch courts, or any
hearts with initials in them. The longer we
skated, the more brazen we got. We skated right
over those dead flies in front of the pool room,
mashed them flat, like pennies on the railroad
track.

5

❧ BOYS ❧

*In 1877, as Kathie Gray was about to turn
thirteen, she developed a crush on a boy named
Jimmie. Kathie discovered her feelings while listening
to her cousin Allie play the organ.*

Jan. 4, 1877

I was sadly sweetly meloncoly last night. I
never felt quite that way before. Allie sat at the
organ in the twilight and sang all the sweet old
peaces that I loved so well in the days gone by
"When I roamed the flowery meadows a little
child." I lay on the sofa and dreamed of other
days as she sung "Darling I am growing old." I am
growing old Journal. Only a few more days of

being twelve and then the TEENS stair me in the
face!!! Allie sang on. . . . "Annie Laurie" and
"Jamie Is on the Stormy Sea." I liked the last one
best of all. . . .

Jimmie is talking of going to sea. Oh How
terrible that would be! I just know he would be
drowned! He is also studdying the telegraf machine
and I am *begging* him to stay on dry land and send
telegrafs. He feels he must make up his mind what
he is to be. His seventeenth birthday is next month.
He is Nature's Nobelman. My *Hero* I call him. . . .

I can write it down to you, dear old Journal
what a lovely, *lovely* time I had today skateing with
Jimmie. To be sure its mostly running on my
ankle bones when I try to skate alone my ankles
are so week but when Jimmie helped me I made
some good strokes. Going over the rale road
embankment I steped on a place that looked like
a frozen snow bank. *Down* I went to my waist in
snow *cinders* and ice. It was a place where the erth
had been washed out and the snow filled it in.

Jimmie came to my rescue and fished me out all
black and begrimed but uningured. He took his
handkerchief and wiped the snow and dirt off my
face and brushed me off then saying he mustnt
trust me to go alone over bad places he took my
hand and helped me so *prettily*. Even after we got
to the rode he kept my hand and walked in the
snow to give me the best track. Then he noticed I
had lost off the button from my cloak at the neck
so he took the pin out of his own coat and pinned
it up for me. . . . Once on the ice he skated me up
and down the pond like the wind. Oh we had a
Beautiful Capital *IRRESISTABLY Lovely time!*

  Jimmie has flashing teeth and an unusual smile.
It makes his whole face *shine*. . . . He treats me so
respectfully—so *gently*—like an elder brother . . .
only I never knew a big brother of any of the girls
to treat them *half* as nice. . . . Then journal—all
at once I knew—I knew I am beginning to be
grown up! I have found out that it isnt an elder
brother that I want—but a LOVER as kind and

smileing and *dear* as Jimmie! Why the thought just frightened me. I felt sort of dissy.

❖

E)leanor Hallowell Abbott's father, a minister, was quite tolerant about his daughter's behavior— up to a point. That point came when a boy started to pay "attention" to Eleanor. This was in the 1880s.

A boy walked home from school with me one day. Not just a boy, as it developed in my parents' minds, who lived next door to me as it were, or even on a convergent street, but a boy who had been actually obliged to go out of his way just a little bit to walk home with me.

It was evidently the fact of his having "gone out of his way to do it" that constituted the heinousness [seriousness] of the offense, for heinous it certainly seemed to be as judged by the measure of disapproval meted out to me

especially by my father. It was all right apparently to play with boys, study with them, kick them, slap them, or even bite them, but to have a boy walk home with one, go out of his way to walk home with one, was evidently that mysterious thing called an *attention* and as such not to be tolerated. Never in my life have I ever known any one who began as early as did my father . . . in trying to prevent any boy from paying either of his daughters an "attention."

It seemed at the time to be the first flaw that we had ever discovered in our beautiful father's character. Once again late into the night Madeline Vaughan [her sister] and I stayed awake to discuss the perplexity of it all.

"But how in the world," argued Madeline Vaughan, "can we ever get married if our father won't let any boy commit an 'attention' to us?"

"We can't!" I admitted. Between drowsiness and resentment all issues became suddenly confused. "But who cares?" I replied valiantly. "I'd rather go off and be a missionary and eat cannibals."

✦

*W*hen Elizabeth Yates was fourteen, she had her first romantic experience, which she wrote about in her diary.

August 2, 1920

Something wonderful has just happened to me! On the space for today in my diary I have pasted four silver stars. Whenever I see them they will tell me of the event that shook my life.

The house is overflowing with people, family mostly. Teresa and Ed [her eldest sister and brother] are here. Walter and Ibby [their spouses], and little children seem to appear everywhere. Jinny [another older sister] has her roommate from Smith visiting her, as well as two men from Yale; then there's Harry and Dick and Bobby [brothers] and me.

After supper Jinny said they were going for a

ride in the moonlight and asked me to join them.
It was beautiful. The fields were so wet with dew
that it splashed from the horses' hooves. The
moon made the world mysterious, and the air was
damp and fragrant. The horses kept whickering to
each other, and whenever we broke into a real run
they snorted and tossed their heads.

When we got back to the barn, Jinny asked me
to rub Belle down so she could go to the house
and start making cocoa. One of the Yale men
went with her; the other one, Brad, stayed with
me. We unsaddled and rubbed the horses down,
giving each one a measure of oats. Just as we
started toward the open door into the barnyard,
Brad pointed toward a little door.

"What's this?"

"Manure chute for the ponies' stalls upstairs."

He pulled me into it, closed the door, held me
in his arms and kissed me! After a minute, or
two, or three, he opened the door, took my hand
in his, and we followed the path of moonlight out

of the barn and toward the house. Brad hummed
the tune of a song everyone is singing this year,
then he said the words—

> *"Just a voice to call me dear,*
> *Just a hand in mine,*
> *Just a whisper in my ear,*
> *'Darling you're divine.'"*

I wanted to tell him that he was divine, but the
words wouldn't come. When we reached the
house, he dropped my hand and went up the steps
and into the kitchen to join the others with their
cocoa, and I went upstairs. In the hall I met
Bobby.

"What's happened to you?"

"Nothing."

"Something must have. You're all out of breath
and your eyes are shining. You look beautiful."

"Do I?"

"Was it fun riding in the moonlight?"

"It wasn't the ride. It—oh, Bobby, Brad kissed me!"

"In the moonlight?"

"No, in the manure chute."

"Oh."

"But I love him! Can't you see that the main thing has come into my life?"

"Aren't you going down to have cocoa with them? Everybody's in the kitchen and they're all talking and laughing."

"No, I can't."

"Then I'll go down and bring you up a cup. Don't take your first kiss so seriously."

❖

Merrihelen Ponce grew up in rural California during the 1940s. The small town nearby had two movie theaters, but only one of them, the San Fernando, admitted Mexicans. Merrihelen and her friends used to go there every Sunday afternoon.

Although none of my friends dated or went steady, by the time we were twelve or so, we made arrangements to "sit" at the movies with someone we liked. One year, George T., or Chochis as his mother called him, asked me to "sit" with him at a matinee. I wasn't too thrilled as Chochis was *un gordito* [a little fattie]. The fact that I too was chubby was of no consequence to me. I mean we didn't have to be *gordinflones* [double fatties].

It was fun to "sit" with George. He ate all during the movie. Popcorn, peanuts and candy. He would load up before the movie, during intermission, and just before the movie ended. To be with him was to partake in a continuous feed. Food was happiness for Chochis, and for me, happiness was sitting with him.

There was a certain amount of security in being with Chochis. He was content to stuff himself all during the movie so that he never had time to get fresh with me. All he ever did was put

his arm around me. One arm on my shoulder, the other entwined around a big bag of buttered popcorn. While the other girls were busy fighting off *los frescos* [fresh guys], I munched contentedly throughout the entire movie, mesmerized by the antics of Pauline and Nyoka [characters in movie serials], secure with an array of Baby Ruths, Milk Duds and Snickers.

6

❧ BECOMING A WOMAN ❧

The most popular girls' book of the nineteenth century was Little Women, *by Louisa May Alcott. Even today, nearly 150 years after it was published, girls find the story of the four March sisters fun to read. Its author, in real life, was a very private person, even when young. This entry from her diary was made when Louisa was thirteen. Her family had just moved into a larger house, which meant that she could have a room of her own where she could write and think.*

March, 1846 — I have at last got the little room I have wanted so long, and am very happy about it. It does me good to be alone, and Mother has made it very pretty and neat for me. My work-basket and

desk are by the window, and my closet is full of
dried herbs that smell very nice. The door that
opens into the garden will be very pretty in
summer, and I can run off to the woods when I like.

I have made a plan for my life, as I am in my
teens, and no more a child. I am old for my age,
and don't care much for girl's things. People think
I'm wild and queer, but Mother understands and
helps me. I have not told any one about my plan,
but I'm going to *be* good. I've made so many
resolutions, and written sad notes, and cried over
my sins, and it doesn't seem to do any good! Now
I'm going to *work really,* for I feel a true desire to
improve, and be a help and comfort, not a care and
sorrow, to my dear mother.

❖

*When Kathie Gray was thirteen, she made an
interesting discovery while doing Sunday school
lessons with her friend Sunny. Kathie described it in
her diary on August 4, 1877.*

Journal I have got to be an old maid!! Yes—
sad as that will be Ive made up my mind this
afternoon and so has Sunny and its all down in
two big family Bibles and signed and witnessed
by Sunny and me. Oh its terrible what St. Paul
expected of us wimmen!

Sunny and I were getting our Sabath school
lesson for next Sunday and as we looked up
references we came to some awful commands—
"Wives submit yourselves unto your Husbands *as
unto the Lord!!*" "But I suffer not a woman to
teach a man—but be silent!!" "The man is to
rule the woman." "Woman was created for the
man" and a lot more stuff! Now Journal no one
but a Namby Pamby could stand for that! Sunny
and I got so excited. How I needed Mama to
straighten things out. We just raved. Then we
got the Bibles and I wrote in ours in the Family
Record where a space is left for marages of the
children. This is it.

A Blank Forever!!!
This space left a blank for the marriages of the
children of Richard and Susan Gray shall never be
filled! This is solemly resolved by Katharine E.
Gray, only sirviving child of the above parties.
Signed—Katharine E. Gray.
Haven, Aug. 4, 1877
Witnessed by Sunny Osburn.

Now isnt that very *legel* sounding? Sunny fixed her Bible the same. I just had to show mine to somebody. I was so stired up, and Annie [a maid] was the only one here. I might have known better for she laughed as though she would have a fit. Then she said "Well Kathie that won't be binding for you wrote it with a led pencil and only had one witness." Huh!

Monday, Aug. 5

Sunny and I cant rub out our "Resolved" to try to write it over legely [legally] with ink for it would *smudge* the page dreadfully. I decided too to wait until I talked about it with Mama before I secured another witness. The Husbands we know dont seem so bad. Allie [her cousin] isnt "subservient" at all and George [Allie's husband] is real jolly when he isnt thinking about Auntie [who was ill at the time].

❖

M ountain Wolf Woman, a Winnebago woman, *told her life story to an interviewer in 1958. She was born in Wisconsin in 1884, at a time when the Winnebago people preserved much of their culture and customs. Mountain Wolf Woman recalled the experience of getting her first period.*

W e stopped at the home of grandfather

Naqui-Johnga. There it was that mother told me how it is with little girls when they become women. "Some time," she said, "that is going to happen to you. From about the age of thirteen years this happens to girls. When that happens to you, run to the woods and hide some place. You should not look at any one, not even a glance. If you look at a man you will contaminate his blood. Even a glance will cause you to be an evil person. When women are in that condition they are unclean." Once, after our return to grandfather's house, I was in that condition when I awoke in the morning.

Because mother had told me to do so, I ran quite far into the woods where there were some bushes. The snow was still on the ground and the trees were just beginning to bud. In the woods there was a broken tree and I sat down under this fallen tree. I bowed my head with my blanket wrapped over me and there I was, crying and crying. Since they had forbidden me to look

around, I sat there with my blanket over my head. I cried. Then, suddenly I heard the sound of voices. My sister Hinakega and my sister-in-law found me. Because I had not come back in the house, they had looked for me. They saw my tracks in the snow, and by my tracks they saw that I ran. They trailed me and found me. "Stay here," they said. "We will go and make a shelter for you," and they went home again. Near the water's edge of a big creek, at the rapids of East Fork River, they built a little wigwam. They covered it with canvas. They built a fire and put straw there for me, and then they came to get me. There I sat in the little wigwam. I was crying. It was far, about a quarter of a mile from home. I was crying and I was frightened. Four times they made me sleep there. I never ate. There they made me fast. That is what they made me do. After the third time that I slept, I dreamed.

There was a big clearing. I came upon it, a big, wide open field, and I think there was a rise of land there. Somewhat below this rise was the big clearing. There, in the wide meadow, there were all kinds of horses, all colors. I must have been one who dreamed about horses. I believe that is why they always used to give me horses.

❖

In 1943, when Sadie Penzato turned twelve, she felt changes coming. She wasn't certain that she liked them, but she had nobody to discuss them with. Her older sister was serving in a women's service corps during World War II. Her mother, an immigrant from Italy, had not prepared Sadie for what she should expect.

The summer that I was twelve, strange, ominous feelings pervaded my being. They made me feel that nameless changes were about to take place. I was suddenly more aware of things I had not heeded as keenly as before. Fussing with my hair a lot more, I even suffered sleeping on metal

curlers! Using some perfume my sister had left
behind I started dousing myself with it, each time
I left for school. After bathing, I reveled in
patting dusting powder all over my body with a
big powder puff. . . . I read *Seventeen Magazine,*
which first saw publication the year I was twelve.
It was my favorite reading matter despite the fact
that its influence on me was not always positive.
It did nothing for my self-image since 99% of
the models were tall, blue-eyed, and light-haired.
I wondered where I fit in, only five feet tall, with
jet black hair, olive skin, and dark-brown eyes. I
cannot remember ever seeing a ravenhaired girl in
the important color sections of the magazine. In
the small ads in the back part, occasionally there
was a girl pictured who had black hair. . . .

Dolls were no longer of interest to me, and
boys became even more important than before.
In fact, they were suddenly the most important
concern of all. Irrevocable forces of nature were
at work. . . . The one conclusive thing that

clinched it occurred that August.

It was a hot, humid day and I was riding my bike over the bumpy and pebble-strewn Jenkinstown road, returning from a visit with my friend, Lucille Miller. Pedaling up a hill made me sweat profusely and my bicycle seat, especially, felt extremely wet. . . . When the wetness did not evaporate once I hit flat ground and was no longer straining, and since I had never before perspired in that way, I became curious. Pulling off the road and stopping, I got off my bike and looked down to where I felt moist. You can imagine my horror when I saw blood oozing out and trickling down my inner thighs from somewhere inside my blood-stained shorts!

For a moment, I stood petrified with fear! Searching my memory, I tried to recall if I had hit a bump somewhere and that it had somehow caused the bleeding. No, I was sure I had not! Frightened, I jumped back on my bike and pedaled home as fast as I could. . . . At the front porch, I came to a screeching halt. Driveway pebbles scattered as I braked. Jumping off, I let the bike fall where I had stopped, the rear wheel still spinning. Taking the stairs two at a time, I ran up, entered the hallway, and started yelling, *"Mama, Mama, oh Mama mia, mi strupiavu, mi strupiavu!"* (Mama, Mama, oh Mother of mine, I hurt myself, I hurt myself!) Hearing the fear in my voice, my mother rushed out of the kitchen, drying her hands on her apron, her face white with anxiety.

"Che ti su-chithi? Che cos' a fatto? A dolori? Fami vididi uni ti strupiasti." (What happened? What did you do? Do you have pain? Let me see where you hurt yourself.)

While standing there I suddenly was aware of where the blood was actually *coming* from. I stood very still and looked down. I was so ashamed. Mortified, I watched my mother's reaction as I slowly crooked my knee to one side so that my upper thigh was visible. I stared at it warily then looked at Mama with apprehension as she watched a thin stream of blood course slowly, very slowly down my leg. The worried look suddenly left her face and she started to laugh. A high gleeful sound, a laugh filled with joy and delight. Indignant, I straightened my leg and scowled at her.

"Mama, Mama, what'sa matter with you? Maa? Are you crazy or som'th'n? I'm bleeding, cant'cha see I'm bleeding and from what I don't even know and you're laughing at me. What is it? How come you're laughing?"

Mama then reached out, pulled me very close, and hugged me hard. I was suddenly aware that it had been a long time since Mama had taken me into her ample arms in this way. It was a delicious feeling to be held with such love and affection. Mama held me tightly and stroked my hair as she put her cheek close to mine. Then she kissed the top of my head and sighed a soft, long sigh.

Holding me at arms' length, she looked deep into my eyes. We both stared intently at one

another for a long moment. . . . *"Ah, figlia mia, si cresceiuta, ora si cresceiuta!"* (Ah, daughter of mine, you are grown, now you are grown!) She kissed me gently on both cheeks. . . . "You are now a young lady and what has happened to you is what happens to all women when they reach a certain age. You are no longer a little girl. Now you are a woman. This will happen every month. . . . Don't worry, this will not kill you. It's really just a pain in the neck, but we all live through it."

❖

Encouraged by her parents to be bold and independent, Martha Carey Thomas, who earlier wrote about dissecting a mouse, became a leader of the women's suffrage movement. Several of her diary entries in 1871, when Martha was fourteen, show how strong her feelings were already.

January 6

After supper we went to Anna Dickinson's lecture. . . . She said one very true thing. She said "that if a boy had genius and talent and splendid abilities, and when he had grown to manhood should come to his parents and tell them he felt it his duty to go out into the world and do his part elevating the human race, they would dry their tears and send him forth with their blessing resting upon him. But if a girl grown up in the same way with the same talent, same genius, same splendid abilities should in the same way express her desire, they would put her in her chamber, lock the door, and put the key in their pocket and think they had done their duty." Oh my, how terrible, how *fearfully* unjust. A girl certainly [should] do what she chooses as well as a boy. When I grow up— we'll see what will happen. . . .

February 26

An English man Joseph Beck was here to dinner the other day and he doesn't believe in the Education of Women. Neither does Cousin Frank King and my, such a discussion as they had. Mother of course was for. They said that they didn't see any good of a woman's learning Latin or Greek [because] it didn't make them any more entertaining to their *husbands*. A woman had plenty of other things to do—sewing, cooking, taking care of children, dressing, and flirting. . . . In fact they talked as if the whole end and aim of a woman's life was to get *married* and when she attained that *greatest state of earthly bliss* it was her duty to amuse her husband and to learn nothing; never to exercise the powers of her mind so that he might have the *exquisite* pleasure of knowing more than his wife. Of course they talked the usual cant of woman being too *high* too *exalted* to do anything but sit up in perfect ignorance with folded hands and let men worship at her shrine, meaning in other words like all the rest of such high faluting stuff that women ought to be *mere dolls* for men to be amused with. . . .

I got perfectly enraged. . . . If I ever live and grow up my *one* aim and concentrated purpose *shall* be and is to show that a woman *can learn, can reason, can compete* with men in the grand fields of literature and science and conjecture that opens before the 19th century; that a woman can be a woman and a *true* one, without having all her time engrossed by dress and society.

Martha Carey Thomas would, as an adult, help to found Bryn Mawr College, which provided higher education for women. She was president of Bryn Mawr from 1894 to 1922.

Text Credits

pp. 3-5: Havens, Catherine Elizabeth, *The Diary of a Little Girl in Old New York*. New York: H.C.Brown, 1919, 54, 56-57, 64-66.

pp. 6-10: Thomas, Martha Carey, *The Making of a Feminist*, edited by Marjorie Houspian Dobkin. Kent, Ohio: Kent State University Press, 1979, 43-45.

pp. 10-11: Gray, Kathie, *Kathie's Diary*, edited by Margaret W. Eggleston. New York: George H. Doran, 1926, 29.

pp. 13-15: Major, Devorah, "Little Girl Days," from *California Childhood*, edited by Gary Soto, published by Creative Arts Book Co., 1988, used with permission, 41-44.

pp. 16-18: *Virginia Magazine of History and Biography*, Vol. XV, No. 4 (April, 1908), 432-433.

pp. 20-21: Raymond, Cornelia M., *Memories of a Child of Vassar*, copyright 1940 by Cornelia M. Raymond, courtesy of Vassar College, Poughkeepsie, NY, 28-29.

p. 22: Vanderbilt, Consuelo Balsan, *The Glitter and the Gold*. New York: Harper & Brothers, 1952, 13.

pp. 24-25: Paxson, Mary Scarborough, *Mary Paxson: Her Book*. Garden City, NY: Doubleday, Doran & Company, 1931, 33-34.

pp. 26-29: Doyle, Dr. Helen MacKnight, *A Child Went Forth*. New York: Gotham House, 1934, 66-67.

pp. 30-31: Woodward, Helen Rosen, *Three Flights Up*. New York: Dodd, Mead, 1935, 45-46.

pp. 33-34: Lee, Mary Paik, *Quiet Odyssey: A Pioneer Korean Woman in America*. Seattle: University of Washington Press, 1990, 16-17.

pp. 35-41: Barton, Clara, *The Story of My Childhood*. New York: Baker & Taylor, 1907, 57-64.

pp. 41-44: Buttz, Rachel Q., *A Hoosier Girlhood*. Boston: R.G. Badger, 1924, 27-28.

p. 45: Richards, Caroline Cowles, *Village Life in America*. New York: Henry Holt & Co., 1912, 55.

pp. 46-47: Gray, Kathie, *op. cit.*, 33-34.

p. 49: Abbott, Eleanor Hallowell, *Being Little in Cambridge—When Everybody Else Was Big*. New York: D. Appleton-Century Co., 1936, 77.

pp. 50-51: Doyle, Dr. Helen MacKnight, *op. cit.*, 110.

pp. 51-53: Cannell, Kathleen, *Jam Yesterday*. New York: William Morrow, 1945, 41-42.

pp. 54-58: Fallis, Edwina, *When Denver and I Were Young*. Denver: Big Mountain Press, 1956, 60-61.

pp. 58-62: Cuero, Delfina, *The Autobiography of Delfina Cuero, a Digueño Indian*, as told to Florence C. Shipek. Los Angeles: Dawson's Book Stop, 1968, 34-36.

pp. 62-64: Cannell, Kathleen, *op. cit.*, 86-88.

pp. 65-69: Layman, Carol Spurlock, *Growing Up Rich in Vernon, Indiana*. North Vernon, IN: Still Waters Press, 1992, 122-123.

pp. 71-74: Gray, Kathie, *op. cit.*, 51-53.

pp. 74-76: Abbott, Eleanor Hallowell, *op. cit.*, 193-194.

pp. 77-81: Excerpted from pp. 71-73 of *Spanning Time: A Diary Keeper Becomes a Writer*, by Elizabeth Yates, copyright 1996 Cobblestone Publishing Company, 30 Grove Street, Suite C, Peterborough, NH 03458. Reprinted by permission of the publisher, 71-73.

pp. 82-84: Ponce, Merrihelen, "Chochis and the Movies at Sanfer," *Southern California Anthology*, 1984.

pp. 85-86: Alcott, Louisa May, *The Journals of Louisa May Alcott*, ed. by Joel Myerson, Daniel Shealy, and Madeleine B. Stern. Boston: Little, Brown, 1989, 59.

pp. 88-90: Gray, Kathie, *op. cit.*, 60-61.

pp. 90-94: Mountain Wolf Woman, *The Autobiography of a Winnebago Indian*, ed. by Nancy Oestreich Lurie. Ann Arbor: University of Michigan Press, 1961, 22-23.

pp. 94-100: Penzato, Sadie, *Growing Up Sicilian and Female*. New York: Bedford Graphics, 1991, 309-312.

pp. 101-104: Thomas, Martha Carey, *op. cit.*, 48-51.

Picture Credits

Kansas Collection, University of Kansas Libraries: frontispiece, 36, 39, 55; Authors' collection: vi, viii, 23, 87; John Hauberg Papers, Special Collections, Augustana College Library, Rock Island, Illinois: 2; Library of Congress, 9; Shades of Los Angeles Archives, Los Angeles Public Library: 12 (Juanita Terry, June 1919), 32 (Easter at the Korean Methodist Church, 1945); Kansas State Historical Society, Topeka, Kansas: 17; Collections of the Maine Historical Society: 19; The UT Institute of Texan Cultures at San Antonio: 28 (the San Antonio Light Collection), 48 (courtesy of Laura Long), 83 (courtesy of Dr. Hildegardo Flores); Courtesy George Eastman House: 43; Courtesy of Milwaukee County Historical Society: 59; Immigrant City Archives: 63, 78; Archive Photos: 66; Museum of History and Industry, Seattle, Washington: 70; Museum of the City of New York, the Byron Collection: 75; Negative #317187, Photo Wanamaker, Courtesy Department of Library Services, American Museum of Natural History: 92; New York State Historical Association, Cooperstown, New York: 99.